He Made Me Do It

Written by Apostle Tameika Sweatt

Table of Contents

Acknowledgment   2

New Territory   4

Meeting Him   7

Request Made Known   10

He Said I was the One   13

First Lady Blues   16

Sister -to -Sister Gathering   20

The Gift   22

Happy 5th Anniversary   24

No More Divorces   27

He Stopped Touching Me   29

His Adjutant   32

Ministry Doors Have Begun to Open   35

Please Don't   40

He Will Not Leave Me Alone   43

His Side Piece   46

The Dream   48

The Auto Show in Detroit   50

Questioning   54

Trying to Move Forward   58

Pre -Trial   60

New Beginnings   62

Am I Going to Die?   66

After all I Have Been Through I Still Have Joy   69

Acknowledgment

Acknowledgments

I first giving honor to Christ Jesus, who is the author and finisher of my faith. I give him all glory and honor for being who he is in my life.

To my Apostle, none other than Apostle Ron Toliver: thank you for being a great leader who pushes me in excellence to be a giant in ministry.

To my Parents, Warren Huggins and Evangelist Blossom Huggins I love you with all I have.

To my siblings Shontia, Jamar, Warren Jr. and Kendall I love you all so much and want the best for you.

To my beautiful daughter Zaiere, baby girl your mom is extremely proud of you and honored to be your mom.

To all my family and friends, thank you for being a very important part of my life.

To the "Golden Girls" Apostle Tanica Bland, Apostle Tania Moore, and Prophetess Michelle Deadwiler, thank you for holding me accountable and being my true friends and covenant sisters.

Last but not least, KRGA (Kingdom Revealed Global Alliance), I am so grateful to be a part of the "Sent Ones".

Love, Apostle Meika

New Territory

I had not been to church in over a year after being so wounded by leadership. I was sick of religious man-made customers. I was burned out from the same old church culture of entertainment. For an entire year, I sat and watched church via internet on YouTube, and social media. I decided that I would minister on the streets. I came to believe that would have greater impact than ministering to a bunch of "church folk" who didn't want to receive change. I remember feeling so bound going to my church home, week after week. I did not want to leave because I didn't want to let leadership down. I was so beat down by the church, I finally gathered the courage to leave my home church. They were not sensitive to five-fold ministry or the prophetic that rests upon my life. I visited "The True Church of Christ International" because one of my coworkers spoke about the great impact the ministry had on her life and community. When she and I started working together over 15 years ago, she was a wild young lady. Since that time she has matured into a mighty woman of God. The first service that I attended was awesome! I was greeted warmly as soon as I walked through the door. The feel of the ministry was nothing like I was accustomed to encountering. The spirit flowed and I felt the power of God. This church was different! I was used to everyone shouting and being excited because of the band or praise team. Never had I experienced a ministry that flowed in the spirit!

The Apostle of the house was powerful. He walked in the offices of both an Apostle and Prophet. His sermon was entitled "The Awakening". He addressed everything that I had been feeling. I looked up at him and said to myself, where have you been? At that, moment I felt like the scales had been removed from my eyes. His teaching was so on point that a fool could understand. Service was getting ready to end when they asked all visitors to stand and give their name and church home. I was very hesitant at first because I did not want to draw attention to myself. All I wanted was to be spiritually fed and renewed. I was at a place where I had been bullied and beat up in the church and I was tired. Truthfully, I said to myself that I did not ever want to go to another church again. I said I would just minister in the streets.

Something on the inside said "get up Monae", so I stood with uncertain countenance. Apostle Taylor said " state your name and your church home". I paused for a minute because I was unsure about telling him that I am a Prophetess. I said, "Praise the Lord, my name is Monae Johnson and I don't have a church home". Apostle Taylor immediately identified that I was a Prophetess. He stated, " you walk in the office of a Prophet. Am I right woman of God? , I replied, "yes sir". He stated that he wanted to speak with me soon, as it is crucially important to my walk. He advised me to stop at the secretary's office after service to schedule an appointment. I did so directly after service.

As I was leaving the church one of the ministry elders stopped me and said, "you should come to our bible-class on

Wednesday." I told him that I would try my best. The elder shook my hand and I left.

Meeting Him

I had a meeting scheduled on Friday December 20th to meet Apostle Daniel Taylor. I never did make it to Bible class because I had to work overtime to cover someone who had called off. I pulled up to the church and there were two cars in the lot. Mind you, the lot is huge; it can easily hold about 200 cars. I went to open the door and it was locked so I rang the doorbell. No one came to the door at first. All of a sudden, a tall man who stood about 6 feet tall opened the door and greeted me saying, " Praise the Lord. Apostle Taylor is awaiting you. Please follow me".

The church was dimly lit. We walked down this long hall, which seemed to go on forever. We finally reached a glass door with the name "Apostle Daniel Taylor" written on the door.

The man let me in and Apostle Taylor immediately rose out of his high back leather chair and said "Deacon Willis, you can leave us.

I will two-way you once we are done, so that you can walk the Prophetess to her car. The Deacon replied, "Yes sir" and left the office. This office was huge, I felt like we were in a corporate setting. His desk was a beautiful cherry wood desk.

He had beautiful Christian painting all over the wall. He had a picture with the Mayor and one with Bishop Lakes. On his desk, he had a pic of him with three girls. He also had another pic of a woman who appeared to be in her early 70's.

He said "Prophetess please sit down. I wanted to meet with you because you need a spiritual father. Not only that, but you need someone to help process you in your mantle". He advised that many walk in the office prematurely and ignorant.

He asked me about myself, my former church and how I knew I was a Prophet. I shared with him that I had attended "Greater Shiloh Apostolic Church". Also that I had evangelized for over 10 years but was called to the office of a Prophet. He asked " How do you know that you are a Prophet? I advised him that God told me and I began to tell him how God dealt with me in dreams and visions and how they came to pass. I explained that my former leader frowned upon Prophecy and did not believe in the five-fold. Tears began to roll down my cheeks. I remembered telling him what God gave me to give to him. I was shot down. The pain began to resurface as I remembered being called a witch in front of the entire congregation. I was accused of operating in the flesh.

Apostle Taylor with tears falling from his eyes began to tell me, "daughter you are right where you need to be." He stated he is not rushing me but he would like me to visit the ministry more and attend weekly bible classes. He advised that "The True Church of Christ" operates in the five-fold ministry and is unlike other churches. He stated that many traditional churches refuse to fellowship with them. This is because they do not believe that Apostles or Prophets exist today. He told me to go on a three-day consecration seeking the Lord on my next move. He got up from his desk and wrapped his arms around me and began to pray in the spirit. I began to experience the power of God all over my body from the crown of my head to the soles of my feet. After we prayed I felt 100 pounds lighter! I left that meeting with renewed hope.

I consecrated myself and the Lord advised me that " True Church of Christ" was the ministry for me. I faithfully attended bible-class, leadership class for the five-fold, you name it. I finally was in a place where I felt my gift could flow freely and be used for the glory of God. I had been on assignment for 5 months and no longer felt like I was at a standstill.

Request Made Known

Friday night we had Prophetic night where Prophet Todd Judges and I ministered. Service was powerful and life changing. After the benediction, Apostle Taylor approached me . He asked if he could meet with me to pitch some ideas about ministry. He said we could do so at "Rams Horn Restaurant"after service if I was not busy. I did not think anything of it ; after all I love ministry.

We drove separate cars up to Rams Horn. Before I could even open my car door he was standing there. He wore his long trench coat, Kangol and blocked off Red Bottom Salvatore Ferragamo shoes. I knew the brand because my ex-husband dressed well, as did I. He opened my door and grabbed my hand as I lifted out of my car. When we walked in the server greeted us. Apostle requested that we be seated at a table in the back, which was secluded. Apostle waited until I was seated before he sat down.

There was silence for about 5 minutes as we looked at menus. I said "Apostle why did you want to meet with me?" By this time, the server arrived and asked to take our order. I will never forget: we both ordered coffee and T-bone steak and eggs. While waiting on our food he stated he wanted me to consider being a teacher for the School of Prophets . The plan was to start it in 6 months. I was so honored and asked "why me"?. He responded " why not you? God has mandated this and told me you would be one of the facilitators". I could not stop smiling as he began to iron out the details and expectations of the school.

Apostle out of nowhere says:" Prophetess you have a beautiful smile". I was so bashful, I said" Me?" He said "who else is sitting here?!" I replied " thank you Dad". He said "you can call me Daniel". I didn't say anything because I was in shock. He began to say he had been praying concerning me. He said God has not given him an answer yet, but he would like to get to know me. I immediately told him "no" and he asked "why not?". I told him I do not think it's appropriate to date my spiritual father. Apostle went on to say he would never disrespect me but it is not good for man to be alone. I bluntly asked him how many other women in the church he has dated? He replied "not one". I asked him what made me different. He said" Prophetess Monae you are so different and just what I like. You are anointed and can work in any area of ministry. You carry yourself nice, stay to yourself and are business and kingdom minded."

After that I didn't know what to say because many of the things he said were things my ex-husband stated. Sadly, after 6 years of marriage it ended horribly. Immediately Apostle assured me that he would always be honest and never hurt me if I gave him a chance. I sat there as our food came to the table and put my head down. I eventually looked up and said "If you hurt me, I will never go back to church again nor will I trust another man of God". He reached across the table and grabbed my hand and said "Baby I will never hurt you; so does that mean 'yes'"? I smiled and said "Yes". I was thinking I can't believe after 4 years of being single I am dating a Man of God who has it together.

He Said I was the One

I am in a good space in my life, my ministry is flourishing and my relationship with my man is the bomb. I never thought I could love again. We have been dating 3 months discreetly and so far so good. This man sends 3 dozen roses every Friday to my office , " just because". I remember on one of our dates he expressed he had fallen in love with me. He said he had been alone for so long since his wife died due to Breast Cancer 8 years ago. He expressed how he prayed and asked God for a woman that would love him unconditionally, and was sensitive to ministry. I reassured him that I would never hurt him because I went through a painful marriage of infidelity. I never wanted to experience hurt or rejection again.

It seemed like since that first date we became inseparable. We would see each other every day. We never committed fornication but strictly PG 13. I thanked God for sending me a true Man of God who didn't break in my house.

For my birthday, this man bought me some Red Bottom Christian Louboutin shoes, a black Saint Laurent bag and a black St. John Collection dress.

To top that off he had me picked up in a Bentley from work and took me to dinner at Ruth Chris' - my favorite steak place.

Oh, I am not done: he also gave me a gift certificate to have my nails done by celebrity nail artist "L", and my hair done by celebrity hair stylist Kimberly Kimble.

I said "babe you did all this for me? "and He said "Yes, the sky is the limit". In my head, I'm thinking that I am glad he owns his own clothing store which is doing very well and also has a best seller. If he didn't have these things, I would think he was taking the churches money.

As we are eating our salads, and waiting on dinner my baby says "waiter give us a bottle of your finest Champagne. I am like "babe I do not drink;" he said your birthday is surely worth toasting to. I look up and I see my mama, dad, two brothers and my son from my first marriage all standing around the table. I asked "what is going on babe?" He just kept smiling and smiling.

All of a sudden, he got out of his chair, knelt on one knee and said "Mo you are the best gift that God could have ever given me besides my children and the Holy Spirit.

Monae Johnson will you marry me and make me the happiest man in the world?" As tears rolled down my cheeks I very happily said "yes". My family was so excited, and my son was like "Ma it's time, you need someone to take care of you.

Since I'm 200 miles away, I feel at ease knowing you have Apostle".

We planned our wedding and decided to get married in 6 months. I told him I never had a wedding and my first marriage took place in a courthouse in Ohio. He said baby there is no budget when it comes to marrying you. What did he say that for? I hired celebrity-wedding planners Legendary Events. My budget came up to $100,000 for everything. I was so beautiful in my $8,000 Vera Wang gown. We had 8 people on both sides which represented new beginnings. We even had Brian McKnight sing at our wedding. We honeymooned in Bora Bora Resort in the Pacific Ocean for 2 weeks. I swear we honeymooned until we could not anymore. We went to dinner, snorkeling, and horseback riding in the ocean.

However, the majority of the time we stayed in that bedroom. After a marriage of 6 miserable years I finally had a husband that is the total package. That man is the first man to ever satisfy me. I know I am getting deep but this man took me places mentally, physically and emotionally that I have never been. I did not want this honeymoon to end; it was magical and exciting.

First Lady Blues

Our honeymoon was the bomb! I was so excited to move into my five bedroom, 3 bathroom mini mansion in the Peach Tree District. My baby had the house decked out; I had to do a few minor tweaks but had no complaints.

We have "his and her " sinks and did I mention we have a sunroom connected to our bedroom? There is a Jacuzzi tub and fireplace and we can see the stars. My bedroom has a master bathroom with a jet Jacuzzi tub and walk in shower. I also have a 52-Inch flat screen that comes out of the floor and disappears with a remote control. I have a huge walk in closet with racks that spins my clothes around. We have a huge theater room with reclining leather seats. My honey has a man-cave with all types of games, weights, etc. I also have a woman cave and I have an office. We have an outdoor pool and summer home in the back. Lastly, I have my dream kitchen that looks just like a celebrity chef's kitchen. I know it sounds like I am all about money; but I have my own coins too now. I am a vehicle engineer designer for GM. I create their electric vehicles and I also own three lucrative beauty spas. Your girl got money too.

Our first day back to church as husband and wife felt awkward. Some of the saints did nothing but stared at me the entire service. Some treated me like I was their master because I am now First Lady. My honey introduced me and let me have words before dismissal. I told the saints that just because I am now the Lady of this house does not mean that I do not serve. I told them that nothing has changed except my last name and my role in their life. I reassured them that I will continue to love the brethren and do all I can for the ministry. I felt led to say that because the Lord let me know some were not comfortable.

As we dismissed, I stayed behind to meet with the evangelists regarding our evangelism team. Later, while walking toward the back of the sanctuary I overheard Sis Jenkins, a youth Sunday school teacher say "Huh she don't phase me, I am still that girl."I did not think anything of it because maybe she was talking about someone else.

I went to the Pastors office and he was just heading out the door. I asked "honey you are not going to wait for me?" He said "one of the deacons is going to take you home. I am looking in a daze because we have always ridden home together, even when we were engaged. I let it slide and said "okay honey no problem". I went home and started dinner: smothered chops, greens, mac and cheese, cornbread and peach cobbler. I set the table beautifully. I always said if I remarried I was going to make sure my husband has a hot meal at least 4 days out of the week. Dinner was on the table and I was sitting there cute and he never came to dinner. I waited until around seven and he never showed up. I called his cell phone, it went straight to voicemail. I went ahead and made him a plate and put it in the microwave with a note. I took a bath and went to bed because I had to be at work early for a meeting.

Around 11pm I heard the garage door open and close. He came in the house, up the stairs and immediately took a shower. He did not speak or anything. I am saying to myself, I know this Ninja didn't walk past me and didn't speak! I sat up in the bed and waited for him to come to bed. He sat on the bed and reached over to kiss me. I asked where have you been? He smiled and said " really dear?" I was like "yes husband". He replied "I am an Apostle and Pastor, I do have ministry beyond the four walls". My reply was "at 11 at night?!! " He stated "I was at the hospital visiting Mother Wilson. As you know, she is battling stage four cancer. I said "I can get with that as I am very sensitive to ministry. You were not at the hospital from 1pm when we got out of church until 11pm tonight. I cooked dinner and you didn't even bother to call. As a matter of fact your phone went straight to voicemail. He laughed and said "dear don't be like that. Some of the brethren and I went out to eat and then to the hospital. Please don't make me pay for the sins of your first husband". I told him "you could have called and said something. I am your wife." He replied "You are right dear. Please charge it to my head and not my heart".

On a separate occasion I remember during altar call one day, I came off the altar and began laying hands. The spirit was heavy. The Lord breathed on me and instructed me to lay hands that would bring about a deliverance. During altar call 54 souls came to Christ and were baptized in Jesus' name. I remember that service clear as day! I was so high in the spirit that all I could do is sit in his glory!

After I came out of the spirit, I looked up and saw Mother Williamson standing over me. She said "First Lady, first lady praise the Lord". I replied "praise the Lord Mother". She said "daughter I've been saved over 60 years". I replied, " amen that is a blessing". She went on to say, "baby, First Ladies do not leave their seats to go lay hands on the saints babies". I looked at her and said "according to who?" She said "baby I am just trying to help you; I have "never" seen a first lady do what you do." I said "mother, I am a woman of God called to the five-fold. If God tells me to do something I am going to do it. I obey God, not man. I am not like others, I don't sit and look cute. I labor, I am a servant of God".

Sister -to -Sister Gathering

Today is our "Sister-to-Sister Gathering". I am so excited to have my baby sister Jasmine and my sister in law Tonya as my guests. Tonya is married to my husband's brother James. It is packed, this year we really outdid ourselves; the room was so pretty! The sisters of the church decorated each table. The event was held in the church fellowship hall, which seated 150 people. The brethren were in the sanctuary doing some cleaning and maintenance: painting, drilling down pews, etc.

My sister kept kneeing me under the table, so I'm like "Jazz what's up?!". She said "why does that lady keep rolling her eyes at you or one of us at this table?" My sister in law Tonya was like, "girl I peeped that too! I am not saved I will tear this joint up!" Mind you, both of them were sitting next to me, one on the right and the other on the left. I told them" pay her no mind that is just how she is". I told them that I had never noticed her acting like that until I married Apostle. After all no one in the ministry knew we were dating as we were very secretive. My sister Jazz said "she is hating for one of three reasons: 1. You're pretty and dress better than she does 2. She's jealous of your anointing, or 3. She wants your man. I looked at my Sis and said, "Daniel has never dated any woman in here!". Both sisters said at the same time "That doesn't mean the women didn't want him"!

Everyone began to eat and by this time some of the brethren came into the kitchen asking for a plate as they were tired and hungry.

I told my husband to come sit down so I can fix him a plate. My sisters went in line to help me. As we were coming back to the table Sis Jenkins was all up in his face. They were laughing and giggling. Jazz was like, "do you see this?" I'm like "yeah and I am about to squash it". I walked to the table and sat my husbands' plate and drink down. Tonya and Jazz had his salad and fruit and sat it in front of him. Apostle said thank you baby and sisters. I responded," you're welcome honey". Sister Jenkins was like "yes, thank you". I looked at her and said "what are you thanking me for? That's MY husband!" My sister in law Tonya was like "Sister Jenkins Imma need you to leave this table boo, cuz I am not saved like First Lady, I will beat you down!". Apostle interjected, "Ladies, ladies calm down. I do not think she meant it like that. The saints here are protective of their leader".

The Gift

I got off work Tuesday around 6:30 pm and was exhausted. I got home and there were dozens of roses everywhere. There was a note that said go upstairs to the bathroom. In the bathroom was a hot bubble bath with rose petals and candles everywhere. I took the hot bath and on a tray next to our tub was a note. The note said after the bath go to the bed. I got out the tub and went to our bedroom; there was a big white box. Inside the box was a beautiful red gown. Next to the box was a pair of red heels. As I went to pull the shoes out of the box there was another note that said go out to the bedroom balcony. I did so and there was a candle light dinner and my fine husband. He had on a button down shirt with trousers and a pair of Kenneth Cole loafers. You can tell he went to the barber because his goatee was tapered to the max. He smelled and looked good. He sat me down in my chair and pulled the silver covers off our dinner.

We had Shrimp Fettuccine, salad, rolls, and Shrimp Ceviche dishes. We were eating and he just kept smiling at me and saying how blessed he was to have a good woman. I could not stop smiling as well because I love to be appreciated. There was a black box with a gold bow on it. He picked it up and walked towards me. As he was walking, he was like close your eyes. I felt this huge neck piece being placed around my neck. My hair was pinned up so I did not have to hold my hair. I opened my eyes and it was a beautiful diamond piece. My husband said "baby I will do anything for you. This necklace had over 100 diamonds in it and was appraised at a half of million". I was in awe, as I never had anyone spend that amount of money on me. I could have gotten it for myself because I do make over 6 figures but I have never been a flashy person.

After we ate, he turned on some Kem and we danced on the balcony. He began to slide my spaghetti strap red dress off. He kissed me from top to bottom. He picked me up and gently laid me on the bed. He slid down my underwear and you can imagine what happened next. We made love all night, he kept saying "promise me you will never leave me and that you will stay with me forever". I whispered, "I will never leave you baby".

Happy 5th Anniversary

It was our fifth anniversary and I was so excited. I wanted to give my husband a gift to remember. I was also excited because with this marriage I felt happy and in love. I am now with a mate who only has eyes for me and loves me unconditionally I went out and purchased my husband a brand-new Mercedes Benz Coupe. I parked it in our garage; and it had a big red bow on it. I prepared a feast for a king. I did Lobster tail, crab legs, loaded red skin potatoes, and a 7-layer salad. For desert, I had a well-known bakery do a strawberry cheesecake, his favorite. I was so excited because I knew my honey had something big for me. Knowing him he could have a jet outside waiting to take us somewhere exotic, after all he is known for that.

He came home and seemed upset. I said "baby what is wrong?, it is our anniversary. He replied baby you did nothing wrong but there is a lot going on in the ministry and I am sick and tired of it. He sat down with his briefcase at his feet. We had an awesome dinner and some wine. He reached in his briefcase and said babe you need an upgrade. He said come here, so he took off my wedding ring and placed a 32-carat princess cut ring on my finger. That sucker was huge! I was so excited and so happy. So I said "close your eyes "as I tied a scarf around his eyes. He said " honey you aren't gonna kill me are you?! as he laughed. I stood him outside in our driveway and opened up the garage. I said you can take off the scarf. As he looked he said "baby are you serious? This isn't the same car I told you I wanted?!. I'm like, "yes babe".

I told him that I appreciated all the monies he had spent on me throughout our marriage and relationship. I told him "baby I would do anything for you". He gets in the car and starting it up, he said " Bae, lets go for a ride". I locked the house up and turned on the alarm. We head out of the gate of our home and take a long romantic ride downtown. It was perfect; we were holding hands and singing sweet love songs to each other. At that moment I said God what did I do to deserve this man. At that moment, I felt free and truly in love with my God given mate.

We arrived home . As we got ready to punch in the code to the gate to go up the driveway , here comes Sister Danielle Jenkins. My mood went from happy to upset. I looked at my husband and he looks at me. I asked "what is this woman doing at our home?" She says Pastor and First Lady, I need to speak with you; its urgent. My husband said " we are celebrating our anniversary. Now is not the time Danielle." I am looking at him like "Danielle? When did you get on a first name basis?" She said "Daniel you better get this straight now or I will". He says come on up Danielle and we drive in the garage and let her in through the garage.

I tell Danielle to sit down at the coffee table in the dining room so we can talk. I offered to fix her something to drink. She said "no that is not necessary". So I asked "what is this all about, did something happen at the church?" I knew that my husband came home upset. Sister Jenkins was like, " Daniel should I tell your wife or are you?" For the first time my husband was dead silent. He had a look on his face as if someone had died.

Sister Jenkins said " First Lady Taylor I am 4 months pregnant. I said, "Apostle and I are here for you to help in any way we can". She responded, "I don't think you understand , she stood up and said "this is his baby!" I was in total shock, and I asked my husband "is she telling the truth?!" Stammering, he responded, "yeah-h-h Honey it is". I stood up, saying "this cannot be happening! I trusted you with my life, you are my husband, my lover, my life. Most importantly, you are my leader!". Sister Jenkins began to burst out saying "he was my husband in the first place! He was supposed to marry me, not you. In disbelief, I responded "what did you say?! She said "You heard me. He was supposed to marry me. He has been my man for over 10 years . He has stayed in my bed! Where do you think he was on those nights that you were looking for him? I made him turn his cell phone off because when you're with wifey (she said while pointing proudly to herself), I require ALL of his attention." I looked at her angrily and said "you claim to be saved and you come into my home talking reckless like this?" Before I knew it I had jumped up and ran to the counter. I picked up the largest knife that I could find. Sobbing, I said "you both have 10 seconds to get out my house before I kill both of you!"

No More Divorces

My husband has been out my home three months now living in a hotel. I really miss him but I will not deal with infidelity. He immediately went before the church and confessed his adultery with Sister Jenkins. He spoke about her pregnancy with his baby. We lost over 100 members. The membership is still large but he lost his true key players. The doorbell rang, interrupting my thoughts . I walked over to the intercom. I say "who is it?". Apostle says, "it is me honey". I let him in and he asked "did you have to change the locks and security codes to our house?". I said " absolutely". Did you have to go cheat and have a baby?". I let him in and walked away from him and sat in the family room to continue watching Lifetime. He got down on his knees begging, "baby please don't leave me, I love you. I will never let you down or cheat on you again. He said he allowed the enemy to tempt him instead of seeking counsel.

I had been thinking about leaving his tail but I refuse to let another marriage be destroyed. I will not be married 3, 4, 5 times. I told him I would take him back if he agrees to go through counseling for six months and does not stay out late at night. He agreed and we began counseling with Pastor Williamson. Things seemed to be getting better.

Sister Jenkins left the church immediately after Apostle confessed before the church what they had done.

She eventually had a little girl and gave Apostle and I full custody. It turns out she never wanted kids, she only wanted Daniel. My husband has no communication with her whatsoever. Things are looking up for us. I began having confidence in him again.

He Stopped Touching Me

It has been 3 years since the baby incident. Our blended family consists of our beautiful 3 year old daughter Ashley, my adult son, and Apostle's three daughters ages 27, 30 and 33. We have three grandchildren who are all boys.

When Daniel and I first married, our sex life was the bomb. Things are different now. This entire past year we maybe have had sex once every couple of weeks - if that. Daniel has been traveling, establishing churches, and Apostolic hubs all over the globe. He is always tired. I don't trip though, because I know what he is doing.

My husband used to love making love to me. Now I can barely get a kiss. I remember clearly that we were so spontaneous, that we would make out in the car, or even at the park. I sure do miss those days. The baby keeps me busy though, so I try not to focus on that. I also seem to have to preach every month somewhere. So both our hands are tired, but I am never too tired to make love to my husband.

My husband just came home from a foreign mission in Kenya, Africa and now he has to go to Ireland. I made sure I had all his clothes and robes dry cleaned. I always make sure my man is taken care of.

The night before his departure for Ireland I bought this sexy ensemble and a cold blonde wig. I looked good. When my husband got out of the shower he laid flat on his back with a towel wrapped around his waist. I love seeing water dripping off of him. He looks so sexy, especially his waistline and six pack. I was ready. The baby was at my sister -in- law's house. I began kissing him. After that it was on, he threw me on the bed and we made love.

He did something to me that was unnatural and I never had experienced this form of love making before. I felt violated and unclean.

Afterwards I felt so bad, I felt like we had crossed the line. I went to take a shower and he was like "Bae, where are you going?" I said quietly "to take a shower". He was like "baby whats wrong?", I told him that I didn't agree with that form of intimacy. He tried to quote that the marriage bed is never defiled. I let it go as he was my head/covering. After showering I got in the bed and he snatched the covers, turned off his lamp, and went to sleep. Months and months went past where we were not intimate. My mind began to wonder "Lord who is he sleeping with because he will not touch me?".

I needed to take my mind off of my situation. I went to dinner with my best friend Evangelist Jackson. She the First Lady of Bishop Timothy Jackson of Montgomery, Alabama. She is my best friend. She came into town because her husband had a meeting with the Full Gospel organization. She and I were "road dogs" all throughout college. They called us Laverne and Shirley because we hung so tough.

Eating dinner with her made me feel 10 times worse because all she wanted to talk about were our husbands. She had bragged about always taking a trip with her husband even if it was a mini vacation to get a hotel. I looked at her and said to myself, I wish I could go back to the beginning of our marriage where Daniel and I had fireworks. We were always with each other. I wished we could go back to when he would have flowers sent to me every Friday "just because". All I get now is him coming home when not on the road and going to sleep. You can be married and still feel alone.

His Adjutant

My husband has been in and out of the country for the last few months. Thank God, he has a strong backing with the Deacons and his two adjutants. He primarily takes his Adjutant Elder Tyrone Jones. At other times he takes Elder Rubin Anderson. We call Elder Jones the inner circle because he is always with Apostle. He makes sure my honey is taken care of at all times. We treat Elder Jones just like family. Elder Jones is a skinny tall dude; he is very nice looking though. The sisters in the church be on him, but he never gives them any attention. He often says his eye is on his assignment and God.

Finally, it's thanksgiving and my baby is coming home. I am going to make sure I lay it out for my husband. I am looking forward to spending time with him, our children and loved ones. Besides, Ashley misses her daddy. The house over here smelling good with the aroma of dressing, mac and cheese, turkey, collard greens, candied yams, potato salad, German chocolate cake, sweet potato pie and seven up cake.

I've got the music playing and my lil girl is walking around singing some old Temptations. I hear the door open and it is my man looking good. I immediately bum-rush him and hug him so tight. He said baby I am so happy to see you. Ashley runs to the door and screams "daddy, daddy, daddy!"

I said "babe go take a shower and get dressed, the family will be here at four for dinner." He said "cool, is it okay if Elder Tyrone comes?" I said "sure no problem, he's family." As he was heading up the stairs I asked " Why doesn't Tyrone spend time with his family?" My husband responded rudely with "because he doesn't". I thought "okay then, it is no biggie." I was trying not to trip because God has been dealing with me. While he was traveling I have had time to have some alone time with God. I sought him for strategy on how to handle my marriage.

I got the table all hooked up .my husband looking and smelling good. He said," babe, I will not be traveling for a minute. He said "I miss my family and I know I have not been giving you the ample time you deserve". I had a big Kool-Aid smile on my face because I had been praying that God continue to bring us closer together. All the family began to come in. We were all clowning, playing video games, monopoly, Uno, you name it. The doorbell rings and quite to my surprise its Elder Tyrone and he's with a beautiful young lady. She even brought a banana pudding for the dinner. I said , " Hello, I am First Lady Taylor". She said " Hi my name is Emily, nice to meet you". Elder Jones said "Praise the Lord First Lady." I said "Come on in and make yourself comfortable". "Honey", I said, " look who is here!" Elder Tyrone and his friend Emily!" Apostle said, "Praise the Lord Elder and Emily! Welcome to our home!"

I went to the kitchen and saw the turkey was done, so now it's time to eat. I told the kids to go to the kids table and the adults go to the adult table. Daniel came into the kitchen to grab the turkey and he sat it on the table. Daniel said" let us all join hands and pray, Elder Tyrone please lead us in prayer". After that, Daniel cut the turkey and we ate. My brother in law was like "sis you know you can cook". Apostle said with a smirk," yes my baby can". Everyone was happy and smiling but there seemed to be a bit of tension between Daniel and Elder Tyrone. After everyone ate, I said "does anyone have room for dessert?" Daniel and I went into the kitchen and brought out all the deserts. As Daniel sat, he said so "Elder how did you and Emily meet?" Emily said " I can answer that! She said, "I was at the Bible book store and we bumped into one another. We've been inseparable ever since."Apostle asked, "how long have you all been dating and do you plan to marry?" I said, "honey now is not the time". Elder Tyrone said "no, it's okay First Lady. We have been dating 8 months now. We started as friends but with so many recent changes, I decided to take it up a notch. We are officially engaged as of today". Emily waves her ring finger. Everyone offered their congratulations. Apostle stood up, and choking, says" excuse me for a moment family". Concerned, I ran into the restroom after him and asked "babe are you okay?". He said , "honey give me a moment I am not feeling too well". So I left the restroom and gave him a moment. My niece asked "auntie what is wrong with Uncle Daniel"; I replied "he is sick".

Ministry Doors Have Begun to Open

I received a letter from The Fathers' House church secretary requesting that I preach at their annual Women's Conference. I was so excited to be on program with greats such as Evangelist Juanita Anderson, Dr. Cheryl Robinson, and Lady Lakes. I called the administrative offices and requested a few days two pray, as I never accept assignments without consulting God and my mate.

I got home and surprisingly my husband was home with the baby and he cooked. I came in and he said "honey what is bothering you?". I said "I was asked to be a part of Bishops Lakes Women's Conference." He said with excitement, "that's great babe!" He asked how long is it for; I advised it is a week-long conference. He said" babe do it". I told him I also needed to pray. So I did the only thing I knew to do which was to consecrate myself. During my consecration, God told me to go but he also told me there will be a revelation in doing the conference. I said ,"Lord my marriage is now getting better and I do not want to leave my husband." He said "Go daughter and feed my sheep".

After my consecration, I told my husband that I would go. I called Bishop Lakes' ministry and confirmed. About an hour later, I had plane reservations, hotel, and a rental car covered by Bishop Lakes. I was only scheduled to minster three days out of the week; the other days I needed God to impart some things into me.

The conference was off the chain; I ministered my three nights and went back to my hotel. I did not feel much like eating with everyone, especially how the Lord used me on the final night! I went to my room, ordered room service, laid in my bed, and fell asleep. The Lord dealt with me in a dream and said, "Go ye home now". I called Bishop Lakes assistant and advised that I needed to go home. She told me that I had fulfilled my contractual obligation. Therefore, I was not bound to stay for the remainder of the conference. Of course, she said, I was certainly welcome to stay if I desired to do so. I tried to call my honey but he did not answer. I called the house and to my surprise, my mama answered the phone. I said "Ma, why are you there?", She said "Daniel had an emergency with a saint and had to leave." I told her I was on my way home and my flight should be there in 2 hours.

All the way home, the Lord kept speaking in a still, small voice; "I will not put any more on you than you can bear". I was thinking, oh Lord my husband is cheating with another woman again. I began to cry and say "Lord I cannot do this". I was dropped off by a car service. I got home and hugged my daughter tightly and told her to play while I speak with Mama.

I said "Mama where is Daniel?", she said "I told you where he was". I said "okay let me go upstairs and try to call him". So I called him and the phone went straight to voicemail. I called the church, I called the Deacons and no one knew where he was.

My mind began to drift, so I had the audacity to call Sis. Jones. Although she left the church after she had Ashley, I thought he must have been back messing with her. After all, you heard the statement "once a cheater, always one". She said "hello" I said "Sister Jones this is Lady Taylor, have you seen Daniel?". She yelled, "No, why would I? I said, " I am worried and cannot find him". She abruptly hung up the phone on me.

I called his adjutant because surely he would answer and know what is going on. I called Elder Tyrone and heard music in the background playing. I said "Elder have you seen Apostle?"he replied "let me go into another room because my baby is singing too loud." He went to a quiet room and said yes I know where he is "B" (expletive deleted) and hung up.

I immediately hopped in my Lincoln MKZ and drove to the South Side to Elder Tyrone's house. I pulled up and knocked and no one came to the door. I knew he was there because I saw his car and lights were on. I wiggled the doorknob and noticed the door was unlocked. I walked into the living room and saw black lace panties on the floor. I thought to myself am like "Elder Tyrone and Emily must be here, Lord why did I come over here?!. There were candles lit and two wine glasses. One had red lipstick on it.

I started to leave but then felt an urge to walk to the back, where I could hear R Kelly's "12 Play" project playing.

I hear Emily moaning. I opened the door but it did not seem to bother them. As I looked into the room, I realized that there was no woman – but two men. I thought, maybe my eyes are playing tricks on me. To my surprise it was my husband Daniel being intimate with Tyrone!

Tyrone, had on red lipstick and a red wig. I couldn't believe it.

My heart dropped as I yelled out "Daniel"! He jumped and said "no baby it is not what you think"!Tyrone in a girl's voice says "yes; I am the first gentleman boo". I stumbled and fell backwards onto the floor in shock, as a panic attack began to grip me. My husband now standing up was fumbling, struggling to put on his pants. He commences to grab me while I am on the floor; I say "Daniel do not touch me, leave me alone!"

In the meantime, Elder Tyrone standing up, put on a silk housecoat and red heels. He began prancing around saying "Yes! I'm so glad you know the truth now!"

That is my man! He's mine! Daniel yells "Tyrone shut up!" Ignoring Daniel, Tyrone continues "I have been putting up with this stuff for years. Pretending like I am his armor-bearer, while you live in a mansion rocking furs and living the life. I'm the one he cries to night after night about not being happy with a woman. I am the one who gives him what he needs whenever he wants it. I gave my all into this and no woman is about to take mines, please believe boo!"

I stand up and began to plead the blood and say "Lord get me out of here!'The more I called on Jesus the more Daniel begged and pleaded for me not to expose him or leave him. I said "Daniel, First you cheat on me with a woman in the church and have a baby on me. I forgave you. Now you sleep with a man?! I cannot take this anymore. I want out of this marriage

I turned and ran out of the door. I barely made it home. I don't even recall the drive. I opened my front door. My mom says" Monae what is wrong baby?! I could barely speak, I sobbed "mama he's gay, he is gay!". She says "what?!, how do you know?"

Helping me to my feet she said quietly " Baby come sit on the couch while I make you some tea"I asked "where is Ashley?" Mama said "she is asleep". Mama sat down on the couch and I began to tell her what all happened.

Please Don't

The next morning when I woke up on the couch, my head was pounding. Mama was in the kitchen making breakfast and Ashley was watching "Blue Clues" on the TV in the family room. I heard the door open and saw that it was its Daniel. I yelled, at the top of my voice: " get out my house! What do you want?!. He yells" this is our house!". I yelled " When you broke our marriage covenant you chose to no longer live here! I ran upstairs and started grabbing his clothes, and throwing them off of the balcony. He was yelling "stop!". The neighbors were outside watching, as though it were a side show. One of them eventually called the police. Mama came upstairs and said to Daniel "just leave". Daniel replied angrily "I am not going anywhere. This is my house, my wife, my child. I yelled " WIFE?! Was I your wife when you were pouncing up and down on a man?!

I kept throwing his clothes out and suddenly he grabbed me and choked me.

Mama tried to pull him off of me but could not. By this time, Atlanta police arrived. Busting down the door, they ran upstairs. An officer asked "ma'am do you want to press charges against this man?!. I said "no just get him out my house", He responded "are you sure?", I said "yes". Daniel yells out "do you know who I am?!"! I am Apostle Daniel

Taylor and I will have all of your badges! The police rough handled him and pulled him out of the house.

The next day I started filing divorce papers. I could not bear the pain that this man has taken me through for the last 15 years. After I left my attorney's office I went to my office I stopped by my office at General Motors to check up on my team. To my surprise I saw Daniel standing near the front of the building. He said "I need to talk to you. You, you are my wife, until death do us part. By that, time, security saw him, called the police and escorted me into the building.

I got off work and went home to lay down because I was not feeling well. Mama had Ashley with her to keep her from witnessing any shenanigans with Daniel and I.

I fixed a salad and a cold glass of water. As I was sitting at the table I felt someone touch me on my shoulder from behind, and it was Daniel. He grabbed me around the neck and said calmly" I am God's Chosen. He will kill you for coming up against me. If you expose me to the churches I will end you." I began to plead the blood and rebuke Satan. I yelled "Satan the Lord Jesus rebukes you, you are not welcome here!" As soon as I stated that he left saying "you have not seen the last of me".

That next morning I had the locksmith come and change the locks and the gate codes. I also went to the police station to file a Personal Protection Order (PPO). While filing the report,

I started feeling a burning sensation between my legs. I thought, " Oh, Lord this man has given me HIV." I told mom to keep Ashley while I go to the doctor, as I was not feeling well. I went to see my OBGYN and they did an emergency exam to check for STDs and they also did some blood work. She said I would hear back from her in 3 days. I had no signs of an STD but she said the blood work would tell it all. Meanwhile she gave me some antibiotics in case I did have an STD.

He Will Not Leave Me Alone

During my lunch break I decided to go to the bank. I went inside, as I needed to withdraw a large amount of money from one of my accounts. I had three business accounts, a personal checking and savings, and Daniel and I had a joint account. I went to draw out what I put into the account, which was $150,000 and told that we only had $200 dollars left in the account . Looking at the expression on my face, the bank teller explained that Daniel withdrew $300,000.00 a few days ago. I asked how could that be without my permission? The bank advised Daniel presented a signed document with my signature. I advised the that I have a PPO against him and would never do that. I left it alone and checked my other accounts to ensure he had not touched them. The bank assured me that he has no access to my personal and business accounts.

I let it slide because I have money with three lucrative businesses and being an Engineer for GM. My family said I should not have let that slide. I decided to go check on one of my spa's " Spa Enchantment". When I arrived I learned that Daniel had fired my best massage therapist. I immediately called the police who locked up him for a few days. His high powered attorneys got him released though. I went home to regroup and saw my answering machine was blinking; it was my doctors office advising me to come in. Fortunately, it was their late day; they stayed open until 7pm. I went into a room and waited patiently. I kept praying "Lord please don't let me die of AIDS". The doctor came in and said " Mrs. Taylor your test results have come back. You do not have AIDS or any common STDs." I felt so relieved. She said "but you do have HSV2", I said "what is that?! what can treat that?" She said, "It is Herpes. Right now there is no cure but we are very close to finding one. For now all I can do is give you medicines like Valtrex or Acyclovir to minimize outbreaks. It can be easily spread. You are also more prone to catch HIV."

I felt so embarrassed, and sad. She said " there are many cases of Herpes. Many have it and do not know it. The good thing is that you can live with Herpes. You must educate your sexual partners about the disease though". I immediately said "who will want a girl with herpes?!. She said "Mrs. Taylor it is not the end of the world". I left her office filled with shame. I even went through the pharmacy drive-thrust for my medication because I was too humiliated to get it in front of others.

While driving my phone rang and it was Daniel. I said" Daniel please leave me alone". He said " you destroyed my life". I said" How did I destroy your life Daniel?! How?! I never told the church about your sins. He said "they are trying to figure out why my wife does not come to church. He said I am tired of making excuses". I told him "at this point I am not concerned about that. You have ruined my life by giving me Herpes. He said yeah, I know I have Herpes, so you should stay with me because no one else will want a woman with it."

I said "you demon from hell leave me alone!". I immediately called Sprint and had my cell phone number changed.

Weeks went by, I had not heard from nor seen Daniel, and I was glad about it. I even received my court papers stating Daniel had been served. I finally felt like things were going great for me and although I was alone I had my Ashley and family. I got up the next morning and dropped the baby off with my sister while I went to go get my hair and nails done. When I came out the shop, I noticed all my tires were flattened. My windows were shattered and there was sugar in my tank. Written on the side of the car door was "B*&#!".

I was in an uproar by this time. I called my god brother who did CCW classes and began taking classes with him. I could not prove Daniel vandalized my car. I felt I needed to protect myself from him. I eventually got my CCW.

His Side Piece

In addition to Daniel harassing me, I now have Elder Tyrone issuing threats against me. He's been saying that if I come back to the church he's going to hurt me.

This entire situation has been so stressful, I decided to accept a co-workers invitation to go to a show. She thought it would help to take my mind off of things. We went to the show and when we were leaving there was Tyrone. He stood at the exit, wearing jogging pants and a "wife beater" glaring at me. "I'm going to "whoop your tail for upsetting my man," he said. I said, "Your man?! He is my husband!"

Tyrone began saying he was messing with Daniel from day one and never will stop. He said I need to hurry up with this divorce process so he could get his coins. I said "you will never get my money!" He replied "oh yeah? I already got $50 grand boo, by the way thanks!" I got so angry that I started charging Tyrone. My coworker pulled me away. When we get into the car she said" Monae I am so sorry you have to go through this, I had no idea". As she was consoling me, Tyrone started banging on her window-saying" "B*@$! this is not over, why don't not you just die?!!"

When I got home to regroup, I called Mama and told her to keep Ashley until this stuff dies down. I felt like my world was caving in and I was about to have a nervous breakdown. The next morning I went downtown and file a PPO against Tyrone as well. I could not believe I was living a nightmare. I was living a marriage full of deceit, hate, and betrayal. I felt like I was losing my mind. I took a break from work to regroup. I ended up getting a room at the Hilton in fear that Daniel and Tyrone would come and try to cause me a harm. During that time, I consecrated myself and began to cry out to the Lord. I felt so wounded and the feeling I had, I would not wish it on my enemy.

After being shut down for a few days, I went to my phone carrier and changed my number. I also provided specific instructions to my businesses. I finally started feeling secure again after communing with God. I had Mama bring Ashley back and plus I now had my CCW and pistol. My brother had heard about all the foolishness due to Mama having a big mouth. He decided to come and stay with me for a few months.

I felt like a person in a movie who was hiding out in a safe haven from a killer. My brother drove me to work and wherever else I needed to go. He would not let me out of his sight. He even hired a security guard to watch over me when I was at work, home alone, or when he had to work. My brother is well off financially. Mama and Dad made sure we all had tuition money and did well for ourselves.

The Dream

My brother cooked me the bomb T-bone steak, loaded potato and salad this day; he put his foot in that food! You know how us black folk are after eating - we're ready to go to bed. He said "Sis, come watch the game. I was like "bro I am going to bed". He said "now you see why the chicken-heads be on me!", We both laughed. I went and took a hot bath with lavender infused Epsom Salts, and fell asleep in the tub.

I had a very intense dream. In my dream, I was at a place full of people drinking and socializing. I had gone to the restroom and when I came out of my stall, I heard the restroom door lock. I saw that Daniel's hand rested on the lock. He locked the bathroom door. He pulled out a knife and started chasing me. I ran and crawled from stall to stall. I was screaming and someone heard me and bust down the door. As they did, I ran from a stall and out the door. I ran out of the building . As I did Daniel somehow came face to face with me and began stabbing me. He was saying that I will never leave him. Now the crazy part is as he was stabbing me his face turned into Elder Tyrone. Apparently I was screaming. My brother ran into the bathroom and woke me out of this horrible dream. I was extremely shaken up and out of it. He asked "sis, what happened?! I told him about the dream and he said "Those fools will never get a chance to bother you I promise. I am your brother and I will always protect you".

The Auto Show in Detroit

I have not heard from Daniel in over three months. We are scheduled to go to court in two months . That is when we will finalize our divorce and custody arrangements for Ashley. My job wanted me to go to the Auto Show in Detroit since my team had created the new 2019 electric car. I told them I would think about it.

When I got home I ran it past my brother and he said "Mo go ahead you could use some time out of Atlanta , away from "Jack and Will". At first, I was leaning towards not going, but after thinking about it, I said "you're right bro".

I decided to go ahead to the North American Auto Show with my team; we could blow all of our competitors off the map. I thought, why not? I needed to keep the Daniel situation off of my mind. We booked a hotel at the CMC Hotel Casino. The Auto Show is being held at the Mercury Center in Downtown Detroit.

Our first day at the opening of the auto show was amazing! We made the others look crazy in our category of Electric Vehicles. We all went to eat at Martha's Place then we headed back to the hotel. My team wanted to go gamble and drink, but I do not do either so I decided to have a respectable night at my room. My plan was to go to my room to take a shower. However, as I entered my room from the bathroom, I saw Daniel laying across my bed. I said "Daniel what are you doing here?! You are not adhering to your PPO". He said "You are my wife. Why would I not be here?!

I said "How did you know that I was here?!, he said, "I have access to all your personal email accounts and I know your every move".

I said "Daniel leave - before I call the police! How did you get into my room?", he said" It was easy. I told them I was your husband and here to surprise you. I showed them my ID and they escorted me up here".

I began to cry and he grabbed me saying "don't cry baby, daddy's here." I said " Let me go Daniel." He said "no". He grabbed me and threw me onto the bed and began choking me. I tried to get up but he was much bigger and stronger than I am. He said "you always were sexy and hot, that's why I married you". He beat me in the face and blacked my eye. He continued choking me and ripped my towel away from me. He beat me over and over. He then tried to have sexual intercourse with me against my will. After so long my mind drifted to another place. I just wanted to die.

I woke up the next day in extreme pain. I looked and he was passed out drunk next to me. He had a fifth of Cuervo in his hand. I staggered to get up then grabbed the steak knife from my room service and stood over his body. Rage came over me and I began stabbing him until I got tired.

As I stabbed him he awoke and said "Monae what are you doing?!" I yelled "shut up" and kept stabbing him. I must have stabbed him at least an hour straight, it may even have been longer. I put on some jogging pants and a shirt, ran to the elevator, and went to the front desk. I yelled and told the front desk clerk to call the Detroit Police Dept. I told the clerk that I had killed my husband because he assaulted and beat me.

A Caucasian woman overheard me and began screaming. By this time I was sitting at the hotels manager's desk waiting for the police to arrive. At this point I did not know who I was or where I was. I was in shock and overtaken by rage. I kept rocking back and forth re-living the severe beating that my so-called husband had given me. I got up, looked in the mirror, and saw a monster. My face was rearranged and blood everywhere. My right eye was swollen shut like I was the one in Rocky Balboa's in the movie " Rocky". I had gashes everywhere in my face and chest, and one of my fingers was severely cut.

My entire body was drenched in blood; I looked like Carrie in the movie "Carrie". I felt numb; I did not feel any remorse for what I had done to this man who took the life out of me. This man cheated on me, gave me a lifetime STD, had a baby on me, harassed me, beat me and raped me. I hated him, he had to die. I yelled out "he had to die!"

Questioning

I was escorted in handcuffs downtown to the Beaubian Street police station. That's where homicide detectives questioned me. I had blood everywhere: even all over all my face from the constant blood splatter as I stabbed him.

Police: Ma'am did you kill your husband

Me: Yes I did

Police: Why?

Me: Because he raped me, beat me, stole my money, gave me herpes and continually harassed me. He cheated on me twice, once with a sister of the church and had a baby on me then with his armor bearer who is a man.

Police: He put his head down for a second and then asked me to tell him what happened last night.

Me: I am the head Engineer who designs electric vehicles for GM. I came to Detroit for the Detroit North American Auto Show minding my own business. My husband and I were in the middle of a divorce. I have a PPO against him as he has constantly harassed me. After the auto show, my team wanted to gamble and drink. I declined as I am a Woman of God and do neither. I went back to my room after dining at Fish Bones and ordered dessert. I ate it and then took a shower. After I got out of the shower I saw Daniel laying across my bed. I said " Daniel what are you doing here? You are not adhering to your PPO." He said "you are my wife, why would I not be here?". I asked " How did you know I was here?" He said, "I have access to all of your personal email accounts and I know your every move".

I said "Daniel leave before I call the police. I asked him how he had gotten into my room. He said that it was easy because he told them that he was my husband, here to surprise me. He said that he showed them his ID and was escorted to my room. I continued to recount for detectives how the tragic events of the night unfolded: I began to cry and he grabbed me and said ' don't cry baby, Daddy's here'. I said, " let me go Daniel!", and he said "no". He grabbed me and threw me on the bed and began choking me. I tried to get up but he was much bigger and stronger than me. He said "you always were sexy and hot, that's why I married you". He beat me in the face and blacked my eye. He kept choking me and ripped my towel from around my waist and pulled down his pants and raped me. After a while my mind drifted to another place, I just wanted to die. After he raped me he continued to beat me. He then flipped me on my stomach and raped me anally. He hurt me so bad. While doing so he said "you never did like this, now you have no choice". All I could do is say inwardly "Lord help me or let me die". After he had his way, the beating continued. This time I blacked out.

I woke up the next day in extreme pain. I looked and he was passed out drunk next to me. He had a fifth of Cuervo in his hand. I staggered to get up and grabbed the steak knife from my room service and stood over his body. Rage came over me and I began stabbing him until I got tired. As I stabbed him he awoke and said " Monae what are you doing?!", I yelled "shut up" and kept stabbing him. I must have stabbed him at least an hour without stopping; it may have been longer. I put on some jogging pants and shirt, ran to the elevator, and went to the front desk. I yelled and told the front desk clerk to call the police. "I just killed my husband because he raped and beat me!"

Police: Ma'am do you have an attorney?

Me: Yes I do.

Police: "You have the right to remain silent. Anything you say can and will be used against you in a court of law. You have the right to speak to an attorney and to have an attorney present during any questioning".

I was held in jail until the next day before I saw the judge; my attorney was able to post a million dollar bail on my behalf. I was free to go until the Pre-trial hearing in six months to decide if this would go to trial. The judge gave temporary custody of Ashley to Daniels' family.

As I was coming out of the jail there stood the church and Daniels family. They all yelled out "murderer, you deserve to die for what you did to Apostle!" At that moment, I wanted to scream and say he made me do it! He hurt me, abused me, raped me, cheated on me, but I couldn't say a word.

Trying to Move Forward

While awaiting my trial, my home became The center of a media frenzy. I could not move without cameras being there. Even at my business, I was harassed. My neighbors called me a cold-blooded murderer. They said I killed Daniel for his million-dollar life insurance policy. That little insurance policy was nothing to me. I work for GM and own 3 companies that are very successful. It seems like since the murder business really picked up.

I ended up selling my home and purchasing a brand-new 2-bedroom condominium. I could not take the media any longer. Although I had to stand trial, I was at peace because I knew that I served and I trusted God. One day I got up to go trade in my car and I met this amazing man, who happened to be the owner of the dealership. In fact, he owns two dealerships. I was at my salesperson's desk waiting on my approval when this man kept pacing the floor. I thought he was a salesperson or something. He had to have walked past me three times. The final time he stopped and said I hope these sales representatives are treating you right. I replied, they always do. He said, "I am not trying to be rude but you are stunning". I replied "I don't think your boss would like hearing you flirt with customers". He replied "I am the boss"I picked my face up off the ground. He and I began conversing and found we had a lot in common.

The following week we decided to go on a date. I chose a place on the outskirts of town because of the trial issue. By the way, his name is Charles Shore - owner of Charles Shore BMW's, yes! He and I began to get real close. He knew I was a widow but he did not know the real deal. One day he came over for a nice candle light dinner. I was very nervous about telling him the truth in fear that he would not date me anymore. We were sitting down eating and he asked "babe why are you not eating?. I said, "I have a lot on my mind". He asked "like what"? I said "I hope what I tell you does not affect our relationship". He said "well as long as you're not a murderer, we're good."

I said "I am not a murderer but I killed my husband in self-defense". He looked at me and said "what?"! I said "yes, I am currently on trial for killing my husband". I told him that Daniel had raped and beat me continually. I also told him that I would understand if he never wanted to date me again. He looked at me and said " I was waiting for you to tell me the truth. It is plastered all over the news. I have heard so many rumors, but I want to hear it from you". So, I began to tell him the truth about everything including my having HSV (Genital Herpes). I just knew he would leave me. He said " Monae I really like you and I feel in my heart you are not a murderer. I believe you are telling the truth. I told him "I cannot believe you trust me" I then said "are you a killer?" He laughed and said "of course not". He and I continued dating all the way up to the week of my trial.

Pre -Trial

Today was the day that it would be decided if I would face trial for the murder of my husband. Charles, my mom, my son, brother and surprisingly my sister and brother- in- law sat on my side of the courtroom. Court began when the bailiff announced "all rise before the Honorable Andrew Pace". I stood in fear, although I had the best attorneys money could buy. I looked back at Charles and he whispered "everything's going to be alright."

The hearing started and the prosecution painted me to be a cruel killer. I could not believe what I heard, heck I never even had a criminal record! The prosecution called different saints to the stand. The one eyewitness that stood out to me was Mother Anderson . She lied and said I was extremely jealous of every woman in the church that spoke to Apostle Taylor. She testified that I would often start scenes. She even said that I tried to jump on Ashley's mom for no reason.

They called Elder Tyrone to the stand. He blatantly lied and said I threatened Apostle numerous times while he was out ministering around the world. When my attorney got up to question Tyrone about the series of events, Tyrone lied. Tyrone said he is not gay and never has been. He said he is now married to Emily.

The prosecutor even called up the CMC hotel staff who confirmed I was covered in blood . They confirmed that I admitted killing my husband. My defense team then went to work. They confirmed the PPO against Tyrone and Daniel. They also had my coworker testify about Tyrone attacking me. They then had my mama testify that Daniel attempted to attack me. This was the longest pretrial ever. I felt strongly that this trial would be dismissed. After many hours, the judge finally called us back in. He said "Mrs. Taylor will you please rise? A significant amount of evidence was presented by the prosecution. I rule that there is enough evidence to send you to trial". I fell down to the ground and yelled "Lord why have you forsaken me?!!" Daniels family began yelling out "murderer, you witch, you warlock, you will rot in hell for what you did!"

My team of attorneys said, "Mrs. Taylor don't worry, we are the best and we will get you out of this".

New Beginnings

Charles and I got closer and closer as a couple. We began visiting churches and ended up worshiping together at a Latino church that operated in the five-fold. Charles was not saved but ended up giving his life to the Lord. We dated for 2 years and ended up getting married in front of our family and loved ones in a private ceremony. I ended up even giving birth to a beautiful 8 pound 11 ounce baby girl. We named her Kirstin. Who would have thought after all of this trouble I would be blessed to have one more child?

I was fired from GM once I was told my case would go to trial. I could have fought it.

However, since my businesses were doing so well and Charles had opened two more dealerships money was not an issue.

I also have a major book deal with Barnes and Noble, whether I am imprisoned or not. This is a million dollar book deal. In addition, I have a 2 million dollar deal with the LMN network to sell my story.

All I could think about is in two years I will stand trial for the murder of my husband and could receive a death sentence or life in prison.

I said" Lord is this a joke?, I am happily married. I have a beautiful baby only to be sentenced to death or prison for the rest of my life? This this cannot be!" I continued to live my life as normally as possible; still serving God in Truth.

In spite of everything that had happened, I still found my way back to Christ. I thank God for my parents. I am reminded of the familiar scripture, Proverbs 22:6 that says "Train up a child in the way he should go, and when he is old he will not depart from it (KJV)."

I may have drifted away from the Lord but I returned each time fighting in the faith. Most people could not endure the pain and suffering I have endured. In spite of it all I still have the favor of God. Charles and I said if the Lord bless us to come out of this, we would keep our business but move out of state. He always tried to stay positive in this matter. I would often ask him: "babe how did I get an awesome man such as you?!

I did not know that I would face more adversity. I was sitting in the California room when my husband said "honey the phone!" I picked up the phone and it was Piedmont Atlanta

Hospital saying my mama is in the hospital. Charles, Kirstin and I rushed to the hospital. Charles waited in the waiting room while I checked on Mama. I came into the room and said "mama what is wrong? She was very weak and fragile. Mama could not have weighed any more than 90 pounds. The doctor came in and said that mama had stage 4-breast cancer and, that the chemo is no longer working. He went on to say that the cancer has spread throughout her entire body. I looked at the doctor and said "chemo? what chemo?!" He said "ma'am your mother has been battling cancer for 17 long years. She is a trooper." I said "What?! Mama what is this man talking about?!"

Mama looked at me and whispered "baby I did not tell you because you had your own issues to deal with". My brother rushed into the room in tears. The doctor told us both that mama was being transferred to Hospice Atlanta Center. It is one of the best hospice units in the state of Georgia. The plan was to keep her as comfortable as possible until her transition. I could not believe that Mama did not tell me; I struggled to understand. Why is this happening during such a trying time?

Mama stayed in hospice for three months and finally passed while I was visiting her. She had awakened and said " Monae you are my strongest, I need you to take care of your brother, he's going to need you." I thought to myself I could get the death penalty. How can I take care of him? She looked at me and said "take my hand", I said "no, mama"! "Yes baby, don't be afraid". She took my hand and saying, "I love you. You are the best daughter a mother could ever ask for" and she gave up the Ghost!

That following week we buried her next to Daddy in the cemetery. I slumped into a great stage of depression. I simply had no desire to live. I had a fighting husband who fought for the both of us. I remember lying there in bed, rocking back and forth. I could hear Charles speaking and praying in tongues. He was saying "Devil you will not have my wife!". He came into the room, anointed me with oil, and began rebuking Satan even more. God must have heard his prayers . I immediately snapped out of that bed of pity, hurt, and stagnancy.

For the next two years, Charles and I were very happy. We loved one another without reservation. I could not to leave the state, but we took Kirstin to the water park and on family outings as often as we could. Charles loved her so much. She was his only child. My son and his wife moved to Atlanta to be closer to me, and with that came more grand-babies. I was at a very great place in my life in spite of the trial coming up.

Am I Going to Die?

It is six in the morning; we get up to go to trial. We left Kirstin with her nanny. I was the last to come downstairs. While coming down the stairs I saw my Bishop, my best friend, and my sister-in-law from my second marriage. Charles, my brother and his new wife, as well as and my son and his wife were also there. They all surrounded me as my Bishop prayed. At the end of the prayer, my Bishop said God told him the jury would find me not guilty. I believed that, but the enemy still played with my emotions trying to get me to doubt God.

The court trial began; it seemed like the Prosecution was out to get me and wanted to see me dead. The prosecution showed crime scene photos from the hotel room. Blood was everywhere. I looked at the jurors faces and knew I was going to be convicted. My attorney got up and called Emily to the stand. I am looking like this girl is on the opposing side. Emily got up and my attorney began questioning her. To my surprise, Emily testified that Elder Tyrone was a brother on the "down low". She did find out that Tyrone and Apostle Taylor had an affair during their engagement. She also testified that Elder Tyrone is still gay and that is why she left him. She said that after Apostles' death Tyrone assured her that he was delivered. He said he loved her and would go through counseling. After they married, she discovered Tyrone was sexually abusing her 9-year-old nephew. Her nephew would come over and visit quite often. She said "Tyrone is on trial, as we speak for child molestation and is out on bail". I looked around but did not see Tyrone in court. The prosecution tried to catch her up but could not.

Next, my attorney called up Deacon Alexander who said he could not allow an innocent woman to go to prison. He testified that Apostle Taylor was making threats to cause me harm. Apostle told him that I was allegedly "going to expose him for something". Deacon Alexander wasn't sure of what exactly Apostle was referring to. He further testified that Apostle told him that he intended to stop me before I exposed him. The court was in amazement. There was a hotel video showing Apostle Taylor breaking into my room. It showed me running out of the room, then turning around looking to see if he was chasing me. The trial went on for a week. Finally, the Jury was ready to go into deliberations.

Every time I turned on the news, I kept hearing I would be found guilty' but I kept my Bishops voice declaring that I would be set free.

The jury deliberated for 12 hours straight. The jury could not make a decision so it became a hung jury . The judge declared it a mistrial. I was free to go. As my family was leaving the court, Daniels' family was yelling "murderer, adulterer!"

Charles and I were ready to put this chapter of our life behind us. We found a house in Richmond VA where he had opened a new dealership. It was a perfect new beginning for my family. I could have taken Ashley but I decided to let Daniel's family have her, I had seen enough of courts. I will never forget that day. Charles, my son and my brother went to get the truck while the women and I packed up more things. We allowed Kirstin and my niece to play outside. We were laughing when all of a sudden my niece ran in and screamed "mommy a bad man is outside and he hurt Kirstin", I said "What?!"

We ran outside and there was Elder Tyrone with a gun to his head. He had stabbed my baby multiple times. I could not move or do anything to help my baby as her lifeless body lay there. It was obvious that she was gone. I said, " Tyrone what have you done?!", He said " Now you feel the pain that I feel. You took the only person that I loved and who loved me without judging me. You ended his life. Now I have taken the most precious thing you to you. Now we're even". He said, "You made me do it" and shot himself in the head.

I ran over to my Kirstin but it was too late, she had bled out and died in our backyard. In that moment nothing else could be taken away. I wanted to die. I began to say "Lord why didn't you just let him kill me? We buried Kirstin in Atlanta, and still relocated to Virginia.

After all I Have Been Through I Still Have Joy

We have been in Virginia 4 months now since burying our baby girl. I still have a hard time dealing with all that I have been through but I still trust God. One day I was at dinner with my husband and started throwing up. I did not think anything of it. A month later, I noticed I started gaining a lot of weight. Charles and I went to the doctor only to find out I was carrying twins and was 5 months pregnant. I said "God you have a sense of humor". At that moment, I felt like Job, I had lost everything but ended up with double for my trouble.

Four ½ months later, I gave birth to fraternal twins: a boy "Asa" (which means "being born in the morning" and "doctor"; and "Alaunas" a girl whose name means "forgiveness" and "healer".

A year later, we started our own ministry "Without Walls International". God has truly blessed us: my story was sold to LMN network and later on, became a movie purchased by Harpo's Studios. I have written two books called "What To Do During the Storm" and the sequel "Surviving the Storm."

Made in the USA
Middletown, DE
19 January 2019